中国歇后语

CHINESE Xiēhòuyǔ

Classical and Contemporary Folk Expressions and Allegories

A Window to Chinese Culture

中国文化之窗

Jing-Heng Sheng Ma

The Commercial Press

Library of Congress Cataloging-in-Publication Data

Ma, Jing-Heng Sheng.
Chinese Xiehouyu: classical and contemporary folk expressions and allegories / Jing-heng Sheng Ma. -- 1st ed.
p. cm.
ISBN 978-9821816-8-3 (pbk.)
1. Proverbs, Chinese. 2. Simile. I. Title.

PN6519. C5M2425 2009
398'9951--dc22

2009016391

First Edition, October 2009

Published by: The Commercial Press (U.S.) Ltd.
13-17 Elizabeth Street, 2nd Floor
New York, NY 10013

Chinese Xiehouyu: classical and contemporary folk expressions and allegories

Author: Jing-Heng Sheng Ma
Illustrator: Keihim Chan
Editor: Chris Robyn
Printed in Hong Kong

http://www.chinese4fun.net

目录 / 目錄
Table of Contents

前言
Foreword

All languages have common expressions, sayings, slang, and idioms. They are frequently used and understood by native speakers but can be very difficult for non-native speakers to understand. These phrases cannot be taken nor understood literally – their meanings are not equivalent to that of their component words. I first encountered an American idiomatic expression when I asked a friend to have dinner with me. She replied: "I'm a bit under the weather today; how about a rain check?" At the time I did not know that "under the weather" was an expression for "not feeling well", and a "rain check" was a way to accept an invitation at a later date.

The Chinese language uses many types of idiomatic expressions, such as súyǔ 俗语 (popular or common sayings); yànyǔ 谚语 (idioms); chéngyǔ 成语 (proverbs); and qiàopihuà 俏皮话 (witty or sarcastic remarks) Among the various types of idiomatic expression the Chinese language is endowed with, there is also a class of folk-sayings called xiēhòuyǔ 歇后语 . The term "xiēhòuyǔ" itself is hard to translate. Literally, xiēhòuyǔ means "post-pause expression". *The Chinese-English Dictionary* (Yuyan Wenhua Daxue Chubanshe, 1997) defines xiēhòuyǔ as "a two-part allegorical saying, of which the first part, always stated, is descriptive, while the second, sometimes unstated, carries the message." Based on this broad definition, xiēhòuyǔ can stem from súyǔ, yànyǔ, chéngyǔ, or qiàopihuà.

Xiēhòuyǔ can be particularly difficult for the non-native speaker to understand. To illustrate, I will recount a well-known example. In December 1970 the famous American writer, Edgar Snow, interviewed Mao Zedong to discuss the ongoing Cultural Revolution. The interview was published in *Life* magazine (vol.

70, "Inside China" issue, April 30, 1971) Snow described Mao as follows:

"As he courteously escorted me to the door, he said he was not a complicated man, but really very simple. He was, he said, only a lone monk walking in the world with a leaky umbrella."

What Mao in fact stated in Chinese was a xiēhòuyǔ: Wǒ shì lǎo héshang dǎsǎn 我是老和尚打伞 "I am [like] a Buddhist monk standing under an umbrella." This was the first part of the xiēhòuyǔ; the second part, left unstated by Mao, was wúfǎ wútiān 无发无天 . Wúfǎ means "no hair (monks have their heads shaved)" and wútiān means "no view of heaven (because he is holding an umbrella)". The word 发 "hair" is homophonous with the word for "law" 法 . Therefore, the implied meaning of this xiēhòuyǔ is "Having regard for neither law nor heaven." What Mao was trying to express was that "he is a man who has no regard for either (earthly) law or (heavenly) principle." This is very different from Snow's depiction of "a lone monk under a leaky umbrella".

The use of xiēhòuyǔ is quite common in spoken Chinese. Its popularity is, in part, a reflection of the imagination and creativity of the Chinese people. People like to escape the dull familiarity and monotony of standard words. The use of xiēhòuyǔ suggests an escape from the established routine of everyday life. For example, instead of saying, "Yesterday's lecture by Professor Wang was really uninteresting," 真没有意思 Zhēn méiyǒu yìsi, one could use a xiēhòuyǔ: [Professor Wang's lecture was like] an old lady's foot binding rag – it both stank and was long, 老太太的裹脚布 —— 又臭又长 Lǎo tàitai de guǒjiǎobù — yòu chòu yòu cháng. Of course, one wouldn't actually voice the second part – it would then no longer be a xiēhòuyǔ, but merely an insult!

Xiēhòuyǔ are also used because they are more vivid, expressive and playful. If one wanted to say someone is doing something unnecessary, one could use the xiēhòuyǔ 你是脱裤子放屁 Nǐ shì tuō kùzi fàngpì, "you're taking off your pants to pass wind."

At times, a xiēhòuyǔ is purposely used because it is noncommittal. For example, if someone is sticking his nose into your business, instead of being blunt and saying 你是多管闲事 Nǐ shì duō guǎn xiánshì (You are really nosy), you could use the xiēhòuyǔ 你是狗拿耗子 Nǐ shì gǒu ná hàozi, "you are like a dog catching mice." The listener will get the message that you are not happy with his prying. Using this xiēhòuyǔ, the message is effectively conveyed in a manner that spares the other person's feelings.

Many xiēhòuyǔ are derived from ordinary experiences. Take, for example, the commonly used expression 肉包子打狗 ròu bāozi dǎ gǒu, "Throwing a meat bun at a dog." Ròu bāozi literally means "a steamed bun with meat stuffing," and dǎ gǒu literally means "to hit (or strike) a dog". The native speaker would know that the intended meaning of this expression is provided by its second, unstated half: 一去不回头 yí qù bù huítóu, "once it's gone, it will never come back," because when you throw a ròu bāozi at a dog, the dog will eat it.

Some xiēhòuyǔ are derived from conceptual metaphors. For example, if I wanted to convey that I have been turned down for every job I applied for, I might use the xiēhòuyǔ 我像是玻璃瓶里的苍蝇 Wǒ xiàng shì bōli píng li de cāngying: "I am like a fly in a glass jar." The second part of this expression would not be explicitly stated, but the listener would know that the unstated part of the xiēhòuyǔ is 处处碰壁 chùchù pèngbì: "hitting the wall at every turn."

Another type of xiēhòuyǔ is based on word-play and the use of puns, because Chinese language has a large number of homophonous words. For example, someone might ask you, "Where are you working?" Instead of replying, "I don't have a job," you could answer with the xiēhòuyǔ 我现在是孔夫子的弟子 Wǒ xiànzài shì Kǒngfūzǐ de dìzǐ, Right now, I am a disciple of Confucius. The second, unstated part of this xiēhòuyǔ is xián rén 贤人 a virtuous person. 贤人 has the same pronunciation as 闲人

which means an "idle person."

Xiēhòuyǔ have evolved from many different genres: classical literature, historical events, popular novels, etc. Of course, similar expressions can be found in every language, including English. For example, if one hears of a young person's death, one might say "Good night, sweet prince," leaving it to the listener to understand the reference to *Hamlet*. In spoken Chinese, cryptic references to classical literature and historical events are common. For example, consider 曹操的儿子 ——奸种 Cáo Cāo de érzi — jiān zhǒng, *Cao Cao*'s son — a traitor. In this example, the speaker would say only the first part of the phrase, leaving the listener to say to himself jiān zhǒng, traitor. *Cao Cao* is a character in the popular Chinese novel *San Guo Yanyi* (*Romance of the Three Kingdoms*) who is a treacherous court official. *San Guo Yanyi* is the source of a great number of commonly used folk expressions, analogies, and metaphors.

As is clear from the above examples, the meaning of a xiēhòuyǔ is obvious only if one is familiar with the original context of the saying, the Chinese culture, the Chinese language, and the Chinese sense of humor.

Xiēhòuyǔ are utilized in daily conversation, in movies, and in literature to convey various thoughts and opinions. However, even non-native speakers who have studied Chinese for years are rarely familiar with xiēhòuyǔ as these expressions are not taught in Chinese language textbooks. There are thousands of xiēhòuyǔ in the Chinese language. The objective of this book is to introduce some of the most commonly-encountered popular expressions as well as the historically and literary significant xiēhòuyǔ currently used today. It is my goal to pique the interest of those learning the Chinese language to explore the fascinating world of Chinese folk expressions, which offer profound insight into Chinese culture and civilization.

This unique book is part of a multimedia tool which has been developed to introduce xiēhòuyǔ to the non-native speaker who has had at least two years of Chinese language training. All materials are digitized and are narrated by two native speakers, available in MP3 format. Graphics are incorporated to enhance the effectiveness of the presentation. I have divided the xiēhòuyǔ expressions in this book into two broad parts: Part I contains expressions that are more popular in character, while Part II contains expressions that are based on quotations from, or references to, literary or historical classics. In each case the xiēhòuyǔ is presented first in simplified Chinese characters, then in traditional script, and then followed by transliteration into pīnyīn. The characters (and pīnyīn equivalent) that are printed before the dash are the spoken part of the xiēhòuyǔ, and what follows the dash are the unspoken meanings and / or literary references. A literal translation for each xiēhòuyǔ is then provided, followed by a fuller explanation when needed, and illustrative examples. In each example of xiēhòuyǔ, the first half is stated and the second half is unspoken, or implied.

This project was made possible by a special gift from Mrs. Elizabeth Tu Hoffman and Mr. Rowe Hoffman.

My heartfelt gratitude goes to both of them for their support and encouragement. I also want to give special thanks to Professor Irwin Schulman and Mrs. Helene Schulman for their untiring patience in editing the manuscript and for their valuable comments. I want to thank Professor Paul Cohen, who reviewed the entire manuscript with a fine-tooth comb and offered many insightful suggestions.

Finally, I would like to thank my husband and my daughters Lyou-fu and Syau-fu for their support over the years.

马盛静恒

Jing-Heng Sheng Ma

2009

Part One 第一部分

Bái zhǐ shang xiě hēi zì — wú fǎ gēng gǎi

白纸上写黑字——无法更改

白紙上寫黑字 —— 無法更改

Black characters put down on white paper – no way to change

People use this xiēhòuyǔ to illustrate that something has already been done and can't be changed, i.e. "what's done is done."

Example

你已经签了合同要买这所房子。白纸上已经写上黑字了。

你已經簽了合同要買這所房子。白紙上已經寫上黑字了。

Nǐ yǐjing qiān le hétong yào mǎi zhè suǒ fángzi. Bái zhǐ shang yǐjing xiě shang hēizì le.

You have already signed the contract to buy this house. Black characters have already been written down on white paper.

Bā zì méi yì piě — zǎo zhe ne

八字没一撇——早着呢

八字沒一撇——早着呢

Writing the Chinese character for eight "八" without [having written even] the first stroke – too soon to say

The character "八" only has two strokes and to say that not even the first stroke has been written is like saying "this thing hasn't even gotten off the ground," alluding to the prospect of a goal not yet in sight.

Example

我跟玛红结婚的事，现在还是八字没一撇呢。

我跟瑪紅結婚的事，現在還是八字沒一撇呢。

Wǒ gēn Mǎhóng jiéhūn de shì, xiànzài háishi bā zì méi yì piě ne.

The marriage between Mahong and me is still like the Chinese character for eight, even the first stroke hasn't been written.

3

Bǎomǔ de háizi — rénjia de

保姆的孩子——人家的

保姆的孩子 ——人家的

A nanny's child – the child belongs to other people

This phrase can be used literally (the child is not hers) or it can be used as a metaphor (something that belongs to somebody else).

Example

这个车真不错，可惜是保姆的孩子。

這個車真不錯，可惜是保姆的孩子。

Zhè gè chē zhēn búcuò, kěxī shì bǎomǔ de háizi.

This car is really nice; too bad it's a nanny's child.

Bàn jīn bā liǎng — méi shénme bù tóng

半斤八两——没什么不同

半斤八兩——沒甚麼不同

Half a catty, eight liǎng – there's no difference

One jīn is made up of sixteen liǎng, so eight liǎng is the same as half a jīn. This saying is used to suggest there is no difference between two things, similar to the expression "six of one, half a dozen of the other."

Example

小蕾的那两个男朋友是半斤八两。

小蕾的那兩個男朋友是半斤八兩。

Xiǎolěi de nèi liǎng ge nánpéngyou shì bàn jīn bā liǎng.

Xiaolei has two boyfriends: one is half a catty and the other is eight liǎng.

5

Bōli píng li de cāngying — chù chù pèng bì
玻璃瓶里的苍蝇——处处碰壁

玻璃瓶裏的蒼蠅 —— 處處碰壁

A fly in a glass jar – bumping into walls everywhere

This fly-in-a-jar metaphor is used to describe someone who is seemingly rebuffed everywhere he turns.

Example

我每天像一个玻璃瓶里的苍蝇。什么工作都没找到。

我每天像一個玻璃瓶裏的蒼蠅。甚麼工作都沒找到。

Wǒ měitiān xiàng yí ge bōli píng li de cāngying. Shénme gōngzuò dōu méi zhǎo dào.

Every day I am like a fly in a glass jar. I can't find any job.

Cáishényé jiào mén — tiān dà de hǎo shì

财神爷叫门——天大的好事

財神爺叫門——天大的好事

The god of wealth is at the door – a heavenly boon

An expression used when hearing wonderful news about money.

Example

你得到一万块钱的奖学金。这真是财神爷叫门。

你得到一萬塊錢的獎學金。這真是財神爺叫門。

Nǐ dé dào yí wàn kuài qián de jiǎngxuéjīn. Zhè zhēn shì cáishényé jiào mén.

You received a $10,000 scholarship. That's really the god of wealth at (your) door.

7

Cǎo shang de lùshui — bú huì chángjiǔ

草上的露水——不会长久

草上的露水——不會長久

Dew on the grass – can't last very long

When the sun comes out the morning dew will evaporate, so people use this expression to predict something that cannot last long.

Example

他们刚认识两天就要结婚，我看他们的婚姻会像草上的露水。

他們剛認識兩天就要結婚，我看他們的婚姻會像草上的露水。

Tāmen gāng rènshi liǎng tiān jiù yào jiéhūn, wǒ kàn tāmen de hūnyīn huì xiàng cǎo shang de lùshui.

They just met two days ago and want to get married, I think their marriage will be like the morning dew.

8

Chū lóng de niǎor — shōu bù huílai le

出笼的鸟儿——收不回来了

出籠的鳥兒——收不回來了

A bird out of the cage – impossible to retrieve

This xiēhòuyǔ is often used to say that something is impossible to retrieve after it is gone.

Example

房客欠了两个月的房租走了。我看我的房租是出笼的鸟儿了。

房客欠了兩個月的房租走了。我看我的房租是出籠的鳥兒了。

Fángkè qiàn le liǎng ge yuè de fángzū zǒu le. Wǒ kàn wǒ de fángzū shì chū lóng de niǎor le.

Our tenants owed us two months' rent and left. I think the rent is like a bird out of the cage.

9

Dǎ zhǒng liǎn chōng pàngzi — jiǎ chōng fùtai

打肿脸充胖子——假充富态

打腫臉充胖子——假充富態

Slapping one's face until it swells up – pretending to have gotten fatter

Chinese used to think only rich people could grow stout, so poor people were willing to slap their faces to put on an imposing front. This expression is commonly used to describe people who, in order to gain face, try to impress others even though they are not rich.

Example

别去那个贵的饭馆吃饭。我们没钱，不要打肿脸充胖子。

别去那個貴的飯館吃飯。我們沒錢，不要打腫臉充胖子。

Bié qù nèige guì de fànguǎn chīfàn. Wǒmen méi qián, bú yào dǎ zhǒng liǎn chōng pàngzi.

Don't go to that expensive restaurant to eat. We have no money, so don't slap your face until it swells up, pretending you are rich.

Dà gūniang shàng huājiào — tóu yì huí

大姑娘上花轿——头一回

大姑娘上花轎——頭一回

A young woman mounting a bridal sedan chair – for the first time

In Chinese tradition, a bride would be carried in a sedan chair to the groom's home. Now this expression refers to someone doing something for the first time, implying inexperience.

Example

我从来没坐过飞机，这是大姑娘上花轿。

我從來沒坐過飛機，這是大姑娘上花轎。

Wǒ cónglái méi zuòguo fēijī, zhè shì dà gūniang shàng huājiào.

I've never been on an airplane before. This is like a young woman in a bridal sedan chair.

11

Dà hǎi lāo zhēn — méi chù xúnzhǎo

大海捞针——没处寻找

大海撈針——沒處尋找

Fishing for a needle in the ocean – no way to find it

This is equivalent to the English expression, "looking for a needle in a haystack."

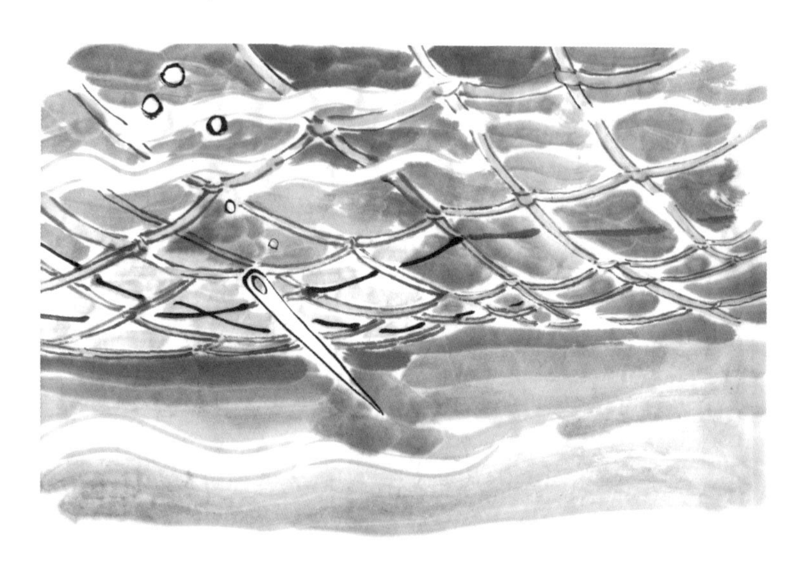

Example

你不知道你的手机在哪儿丢的。我上哪儿找？这是大海捞针嘛。

你不知道你的手機在哪兒丟的。我上哪兒找？這是大海撈針嘛。

Nǐ bù zhīdao nǐ de shǒujī zài nǎr diū de. Wǒ shàng nǎr zhǎo? Zhè shì dà hǎi lāo zhēn ma.

You don't know where you lost your cell phone. Where should I look? It's like fishing for a needle in the ocean.

Dà pào dǎ cāngying — dà cái xiǎo yòng

大炮打苍蝇——大才小用

大炮打蒼蠅——大才小用

Shooting at a fly with a cannon – using talented people for trivial, insignificant tasks

A cannon is used to shoot something huge, certainly not something as small as a fly. Thus this expression is used to say one shouldn't waste someone's talent on a trivial matter.

Example

沈大夫在中国是有名的医生，现在在美国做保姆。这真是大炮打苍蝇！

沈大夫在中國是有名的醫生，現在在美國做保姆。這真是大炮打蒼蠅！

Shěn dàifu zài Zhōngguó shì yǒumíng de yīshēng, xiànzài zài Měiguó zuò bǎomǔ. Zhè zhēn shì dà pào dǎ cāngying!

Dr. Shen was a famous doctor in China, now she's a nanny in the United States. It's like shooting a fly with a cannon!

13

Dāng yì tiān héshang zhuàng yì tiān zhōng — dé guò qiě guò

当一天和尚撞一天钟——得过且过

當一天和尚撞一天鐘——得過且過

Go on tolling the bell as long as one is a monk – muddling along

This expression is used to describe someone who has a passive attitude toward life or work; in other words, someone who is just marking time.

Example

他对他的工作没兴趣。他只是当一天和尚撞一天钟。

他對他的工作沒興趣。他只是當一天和尚撞一天鐘。

Tā duì tāde gōngzuò méi xìngqù. Tā zhǐ shì dāng yì tiān héshang zhuàng yì tiān zhōng.

He is not interested in his job. He's just like a monk tolling the bell every day.

14

Dāozi kǒu dòufu xīn — zuǐ yìng xīn ruǎn

刀子口，豆腐心——嘴硬心软

刀子口，豆腐心——嘴硬心軟

Mouth like a knife, heart like bean curd – a sharp tongue, but a soft heart

This expression is used to describe someone who speaks harsh words but he or she is kind-hearted.

Example

他是刀子口，豆腐心。他骂你以后会原谅你的。

他是刀子口，豆腐心。他罵你以後會原諒你的。

Tā shì dāozi kǒu, dòufu xīn. Tā mà nǐ yǐhòu huì yuánliàng nǐ de.

He has a mouth like a knife, but a heart like bean curd. He will forgive you after he scolds you.

15

Děng gōngjī xià dàn — méiyǒu zhǐwàng

等公鸡下蛋——没有指望

等公雞下蛋——沒有指望

Waiting for a rooster to lay eggs – hopeless situation

This expression is used to describe a hopeless situation or something which will never come true.

Example

张医生说他们不可能有孩子了，可是他们不相信，我看他们是等公鸡下蛋。

張醫生說他們不可能有孩子了，可是他們不相信，我看他們是等公雞下蛋。

Zhāng yīshēng shuō tāmen bù kěnéng yǒu háizi le, kěshì tāmen bù xiāngxìn, wǒ kàn tāmen shì děng gōngjī xià dàn.

Dr. Zhang said they can't have any children, but they refuse to believe it. I think they're waiting for a rooster to lay eggs.

Diànxiàn gān shang bǎng jīmáo — hǎo dà de [dǎnzi] dǎnzi

电线竿上绑鸡毛——好大的〔掸子〕胆子！

電線竿上綁雞毛——好大的〔撣子〕膽子！

Tying chicken feathers on a utility pole – what a lot of [feather duster] nerve

Dǎnzi 掸子 "duster" is a pun on dǎnzi 胆子 "gall, or nerve." A mocking way to say that someone has a lot of nerve.

Example

你把你父亲的钱偷去玩股票了。你真是电线竿上绑鸡毛！

你把你父親的錢偷去玩股票了。你真是電線竿上綁雞毛！

Nǐ bǎ nǐ fùqin de qián tōu qù wán gǔpiào le. Nǐ zhēn shì diànxiàn gān shang bǎng jīmáo!

You stole your father's money to speculate in stocks. You really are tying chicken feathers to a utility pole!

17

Duàn le xiàn de fēngzheng — bù zhī qù xiàng

断了线的风筝——不知去向

斷了線的風箏——不知去向

A kite with a broken string – don't know where it went

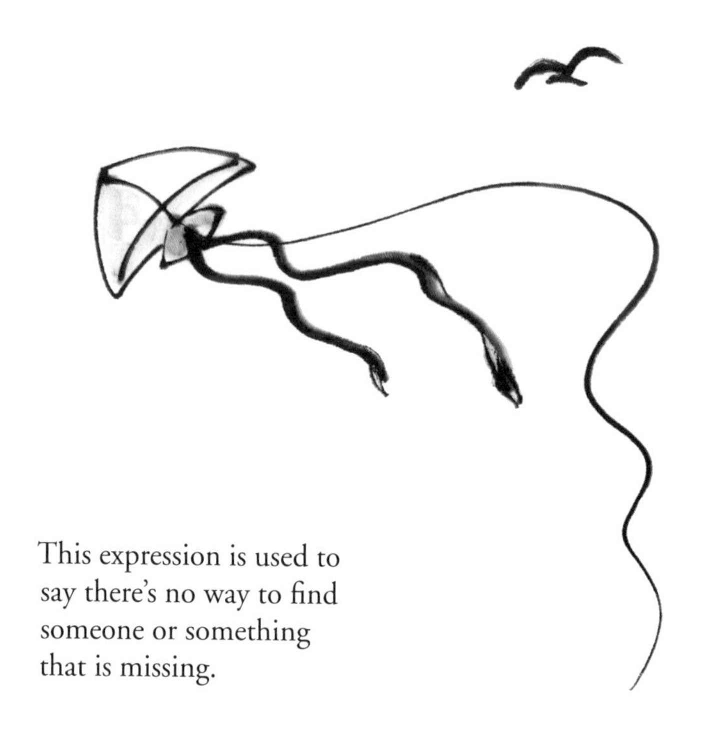

This expression is used to say there's no way to find someone or something that is missing.

Example

玛丽去美国以后就一直没有消息，像是断了线的风筝了。

瑪麗去美國以後就一直沒有消息，像是斷了線的風箏了。

Mǎlì qù Měiguó yǐhòu jiù yìzhí méiyǒu xiāoxi, xiàng shì duàn le xiàn de fēngzheng le.

We've not heard from Mary since she left for the United States. She's like a kite with a broken string.

Fēijī shang liáotiān — kōng tán

飞机上聊天——空谈

飛機上聊天——空談

Chatting aboard an airplane – empty talk

kōng 空 can either mean "sky" or "empty." Liáotiān has the same meaning as tánhuà = chat. This xiēhòuyǔ is a play on the two meanings of kōng tán: "talking in the sky" and "empty talk."

Example

你们这些学者一天到晚所谈的理论都像是在飞机上聊天儿。

你們這些學者一天到晚所談的理論都像是在飛機上聊天兒。

Nǐmen zhè xiē xuézhě yìtiān dào wǎn suǒ tán de lǐlùn dōu xiàng shì zài fēijī shang liáotiānr.

The theories you scholars talk about is the same as talking on an airplane all day long.

19

Fēijī shang diǎn dēng — gāomíng

飞机上点灯——高明

飛機上點燈 —— 高明

A light on the airplane – [high brightness] a brilliant idea

This xiēhòuyǔ plays on the fact that gāomíng 高明 literally means "high brightness," also is used to mean brilliant in the sense of really clever.

Example

大家都说你这个主意是飞机上点灯。

大家都說你這個主意是飛機上點燈。

Dàjiā dōu shuō nǐ zhège zhǔyi shì fēijī shang diǎn dēng.

Everyone says this idea of yours is like lighting a lamp on an airplane.

Fēi'é pū huǒ — zì qǔ mièwáng

飞蛾扑火—自取灭亡

飛蛾撲火 — 自取滅亡

Like a moth to a flame – inviting self-destruction

20

This xiēhòuyǔ is used to describe someone who is bringing disaster on himself or is following his own road to ruin.

Example

张三抽很多大麻，真是飞蛾扑火。

張三抽很多大麻，真是飛蛾撲火。

Zhāng Sān chōu hěn duō dàmá, zhēn shì fēi'é pū huǒ.

Zhang San smokes a lot of marijuana. He's like a moth to a flame.

21

Fēng chuī dēnglong — yáobǎi bú dìng

风吹灯笼——摇摆不定

風吹燈籠 —— 搖擺不定

The wind blowing a lantern – wavering unsteadily

Chinese lanterns are made of paper. When the wind blows the lantern, it will sway back and forth instead of remaining still. This expression is used to describe someone whose views or loyalties are wavering.

Example

你不可以像风吹灯笼啊！一天你要嫁给他，第二天又改变主意了。

你不可以像風吹燈籠啊！一天你要嫁給他，第二天又改變主意了。

Nǐ bù kěyǐ xiàng fēng chuī dēnglong a! Yìtiān nǐ yào jià gěi tā, dì'èrtiān yòu gǎibiàn zhǔyi le.

You can't be like a lantern in the wind. One day you want to marry him and the next day you change your mind.

Gěi sǐrén yī bìng — báifèi gōngfu

给死人医病——白费功夫

給死人醫病 ——白費功夫

Giving medical treatment to the dead – something done in vain

This expression is used to say that an effort or action is pointless.

Example

你们把意见告诉学校就跟给死人治 / 医病一样，根本没有人会看你们的意见。

你們把意見告訴學校就跟給死人治 / 醫病一樣，根本沒有人會看你們的意見。

Nǐmen bǎ yìjiàn gàosu xuéxiào jiù gēn gěi sǐrén zhì / yī bìng yíyàng, gēnběn méiyǒu rén huì kàn nǐmen de yìjiàn.

Conveying your suggestions to the school is like giving medical treatment to the dead. No one will read your suggestions.

23

Gé nián de huánglì — guò shí le

隔年的皇历——过时了

隔年的皇曆——過時了

Last year's almanac – out of date

Huangli is a colloquial term for almanac or calendar. Last year's calendar is useless. This xiēhòuyǔ is used to describe something that is out of date and consequently valueless.

三吋磁盘已是隔年的皇历，现在谁都不用了。

三吋磁盤已是隔年的皇曆，現在誰都不用了。

Sān cùn cípán yǐ shì gé nián de huánglì, xiànzài shéi dōu bú yòng le.

The 3-inch disk has become last year's almanac and it is not used anymore.

Guà yángtóu, mài gǒu ròu — míng bù fú shí huò shì yǒu míng wúshí

挂羊头，卖狗肉——名不符实或是有名无实

掛羊頭，賣狗肉——名不符實或是有名無實

Hanging up a sheep's head and selling dog's meat – the name doesn't match the actuality or exists only in name

Some Chinese butcher shops hang the meat they sell. Dog's meat is cheaper than mutton, so this expression is used to describe someone who peddles an inferior product by advertising it as a quality one.

Example

别相信他们的广告。我听说他们是挂羊头，卖狗肉。

別相信他們的廣告。我聽說他們是掛羊頭，賣狗肉。

Bié xiāngxìn tāmen de guǎnggào. Wǒ tīng shuō tāmen shì guà yángtóu, mài gǒu ròu.

Don't believe their advertisements. I've heard that they're hanging up a sheep's head and selling dog meat.

25

Guāncai li shēn shǒu — sǐ yào qián

棺材里伸手——死要钱

棺材裏伸手——死要錢

A [dead person's] hand reaching out of a coffin – asking for money after one dies; overly greedy for money

This expression is used to describe someone overly greedy for money. The word 死 sǐ means "die"; but it also means "extremely, overly."

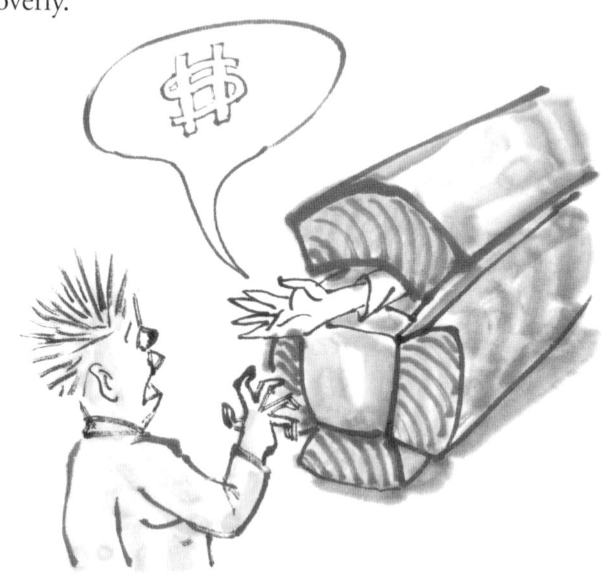

Example

现在我们的政府又要加税了，真是棺材里伸手。

現在我們的政府又要加稅了，真是棺材裏伸手。

Xiànzài wǒmen de zhèngfǔ yòu yào jiā shuì le, zhēn shì guāncai li shēn shǒu.

Now our government is going to increase taxes again. It's really like a [dead person's] hand reaching out of the coffin.

Guāncai shang huà lǎohǔ — xià sǐ rén

棺材上画老虎——吓死人

26

棺材上畫老虎——嚇死人

Painting a tiger on a coffin – to frighten the dead; extremely frightened

This expression is a word-play – xià sǐrén "to frighten the dead" is a pun on xià sǐ rén "frightened to death." It is used to describe something which is very scary or someone who has been severely frightened.

Example

那个电影是棺材上画老虎。别带小孩子去看。

那個電影是棺材上畫老虎。別帶小孩子去看。

Nèige diànyǐng shì guāncai shang huà lǎohǔ. Bié dài xiǎoháizi qù kàn.

That movie is painting a tiger on a coffin. Don't take little kids to watch it.

27

Gǒu gǎibuliǎo chī shǐ — běnxìng nán yí
狗改不了吃屎——本性难移

狗改不了吃屎 —— 本性難移

Dogs can't keep from eating excrement – it's hard to change one's nature

This expression is used to say that to change one's nature is difficult. It is simil
to the English expression, "A leopard won't change its spots," or, in the examp
below, "Once a thief. always a thief."

If you don't believe this xiēhòuyǔ, please read the following passage from 杨
Yang Jiang 干校六记 , translated by Howard Goldblatt as Six Chapters from M
Life "Downunder", Seattle, University of Washington Press, etc., p. 53

"One day A-xiang walked over with a bashful look on her face and whisper
in my ear: 'I've got something to tell you.' Then she laughed an embarrass
laugh, finally saying: 'Quickie [a puppy]... did you know? She's in the outhouse
eating... excrement!' I laughed in spite of myself. 'The way you look, I thoug
for a minute it was you who was eating it!' But A-xiang was worried: 'She
getting used to it, so what are we going to do? It's filthy!' I told her that ever
dog in the village ate excrement. Shortly after my daughter had arrived i
the countryside, a baby who slept on the same earthen kang had had a bow
movement right on the bed mat, which my flustered daughter tried to clean u
with a handful of toilet paper. One of the village women ran up and rebuked he
over wasting not only the toilet paper but the excrement as well. Then she calle
out, 'Wu – lu, lu, lu, Iu,' after which a dog came rushing in, jumped up ont
the kang, and began licking at the mess, licking it all clean, including the baby
buttocks.There was no need to wash it off or wipe it clean. So every mornin
when I heard my neighbors calling their dogs with shouts of 'Wu – lu, lu, lu, lu
I knew that their babies were feeding the family dogs."

Example

老王的儿子刚从监狱出来，昨天又偷东西，让警察抓起来了。真是狗改不了吃屎。

老王的兒子剛從監獄出來，昨天又偷東西，讓警察抓起來了。真是狗改不了吃屎。

Lǎo Wáng de érzi gāng cóng jiānyù chūlai, zuótiān yòu tōu dōngxi, ràng jǐngchá zhuā qilai le. Zhēn shì gǒu gǎibuliǎo chī shǐ.

Lao Wang's son just got out of jail and yesterday he once again stole something, which resulted in his being arrested by the police. He is really like a dog that can't stop eating excrement.

Gǒu zuǐ li tǔ bù chū xiàngyá — méi hǎo huà

狗嘴里吐不出象牙——没好话

狗嘴裏吐不出象牙 ——沒好話

No ivory tusk comes from a dog's mouth – having an uncivil tongue

This expression is used to describe someone who can't use decent language: what can you expect from a dog but a bark?

Example

你不能相信他说的话。狗嘴里是吐不出象牙的 。

你不能相信他說的話。狗嘴裏是吐不出象牙的 。

Nǐ bù néng xiāngxìn tā shuō de huà. Gǒu zuǐ li shì tǔ bù chū xiàngyá de.

You can't believe what he said. No ivory tusk comes from a dog's mouth.

29

Gǒu ná hàozi — duō guǎn xiánshì

狗拿耗子——多管闲事

狗拿耗子——多管閒事

A dog trying to catch mice – poking one's nose into other people's business

It's a cat's job to catch mice, not a dog's. This expression is used to describe a busybody who is always interfering in other people's affairs.

Example

你是狗拿耗子。你姐姐离婚是她自己的事，用不着你管。

你是狗拿耗子。你姐姐離婚是她自己的事，用不着你管。

Nǐ shì gǒu ná hàozi. Nǐ jiějie líhūn shì tā zìjǐ de shì, yòng bù zháo nǐ guǎn.

You are just like a dog catching mice. If your elder sister wants to get a divorce it's her business; you don't need to meddle.

Guò jiē lǎoshǔ — rénrén hǎn dǎ

过街老鼠——人人喊打

過街老鼠 —— 人人喊打

A rat crossing the street – everyone yells at it and beats it

People don't like rats so when they see a rat crossing the street, they scream, "Kill the rat!" This xiēhòuyǔ also implies everyone hits a man only when he's down.

Example

那强奸犯从法院被押到监狱时，就像过街老鼠一样。

那強姦犯從法院被押到監獄時，就像過街老鼠一樣。

Nà qiángjiān fàn cóng fǎyuàn bèi yā dào jiānyù shí, jiù xiàng guò jiē lǎoshǔ yíyàng.

The criminal who was found guilty of rape was like a rat crossing the street when he was moved from the Court to the prison.

31

Hǎi dǐ lāo yuè — báifèi shì

海底捞月——白费事

海底撈月——白費事

Fishing for the moon in the sea – a vain effort

This expression described an effort which is ultimately pointless.

Example

你没有他的地址，也不知道他的电话号码，到哪儿找去？你这不是海底捞月吗？

你沒有他的地址，也不知道他的電話號碼，到哪兒找去？你這不是海底撈月嗎？

Nǐ méiyǒu tā de dìzhǐ, yě bù zhīdao tā de diànhuà hàomǎ, dào nǎr zhǎo qu? Nǐ zhè bú shì hǎi dǐ lāo yuè ma?

You don't have his address or his phone number. Where will you go to find him? Aren't you like fishing for the moon in the sea?

Huángshǔláng gěi jī bàinián — bù huái hǎoyì

黄鼠狼给鸡拜年——不怀好意

黄鼠狼給雞拜年 —— 不懷好意

A yellow weasel wishing Happy New Year to a chicken – harboring no good intentions

If a weasel pays a chicken a New Year's visit, obviously it has an ulterior motive. This xiēhòuyǔ is used to characterize a hypocrite, who acts kind but is actually vicious.

Example

我看他们是黄鼠狼给鸡拜年。你最好别见他们。

我看他們是黄鼠狼給雞拜年。你最好别見他們。

Wǒ kàn tāmen shì huángshǔláng gěi jī bàinián. Nǐ zuì hǎo bié jiàn tāmen.

I think they are yellow weasels wishing a chicken Happy New Year: you'd better not see them.

33

Hǔ tóu shé wěi — yǒu shǐ wú zhōng

虎头蛇尾——有始无终

虎頭蛇尾——有始無終

The head of a tiger and the tail of a snake – having a strong beginning but a weak ending

This expression is used to describe someone starting something well but finishing poorly.

Example

我们做事想要成功，绝对不可以虎头蛇尾。

我們做事想要成功，絕對不可以虎頭蛇尾。

Wǒmen zuòshì xiǎng yào chénggōng, juéduì bù kěyǐ hǔ tóu shé wěi.

If we want to succeed, we must not be like the head of a tiger and the tail of a snake.

Huǒ shāo méimao — zhǐ gù yǎnqián

火烧眉毛——只顾眼前

火燒眉毛——只顧眼前

The fire is singeing their eyebrows – can only take care of what is in front of them

This xiēhòuyǔ is used when circumstances are extremely urgent and the most pressing problems must be dealt with first, leaving less-important matters for later.

Example

我现在是火烧眉毛。无法作长久的计划。

我現在是火燒眉毛。無法作長久的計劃。

Wǒ xiànzài shì huǒ shāo méimao. Wúfǎ zuò chángjiǔ de jìhuà.

Right now the fire is singeing my eyebrows. I can't make long-term plans.

35

Huánglián shù xià tán qín — kǔ zhōng zuò lè

黄连树下弹琴——苦中作樂

黃連樹下彈琴——苦中作樂

Playing the qin under a Chinese goldthread tree – seeking pleasure amid bitterness

The Chinese goldthread tree produces a bitter herb used in Chinese medicine. The qín is a seven-stringed musical instrument. This expression is used to describe someone who tries to be happy even under bitter circumstances.

Example

你失业了，还能在黄连树下弹琴啊！

你失業了，還能在黃連樹下彈琴啊！

Nǐ shīyè le, hái néng zài huánglián shù xià tán qín a!

You have lost your job but can still play the qin under a goldthread tree!

Jī fēi le, dàn dǎ le — liǎng tóu luò kōng

鸡飞了，蛋打了——两頭落空

鷄飛了，蛋打了——兩頭落空

The hen has flown off and the eggs have broken – to lose both ways

This expression is used to describe someone who tried to achieve two goals but in the end gained neither; or, as in the example below, someone who gives up something for the sake of something better, but ends in losing the one without gaining the other. Similar to "Out of the frying pan, into the fire."

Example

玛丽把这儿的工作辞了去美国找事，到现在还没找到工作，听说她生活很困难。真是鸡飞了，蛋打了。

瑪麗把這兒的工作辭了去美國找事，到現在還沒找到工作，聽說她生活很困難。真是雞飛了，蛋打了。

Mǎlì bǎ zhèr de gōngzuò cí le qù Měiguó zhǎoshì, dào xiànzài hái méi zhǎodào gōngzuò, tīng shuō tā shēnghuó hěn kùnnan. Zhēn shì jī fēi le, dàn dǎ le.

Mary quit her job here and went to America to look for work. She still hasn't found anything, and I've heard she's having a hard time there. This really is a case of "the hen has flown away and the eggs have broken."

37

Jīdàn lǐtou tiāo gǔtou — zhǎo chá

鸡蛋里头挑骨头——找碴

雞蛋裏頭挑骨頭 —— 找碴

Looking for bones in an egg – looking for fault

Someone who tries to pick bones out of an egg is trying to find something that is not there. This expression is used to refer to someone who is hypercritical and likes to find fault where it can't be found.

Example

我这个老板总喜欢鸡蛋里头挑骨头。

我這個老闆總喜歡雞蛋裏頭挑骨頭。

Wǒ zhège lǎobǎn zǒng xǐhuan jīdàn lǐtou tiāo gǔtou.

This boss of mine always likes looking for bones in an egg.

Jíjīngfēng yùjiàn màn lángzhōng — nǐ jí tā bù jí
急惊风遇见慢郎中——你急他不急

急驚風遇見慢郎中 ——你急他不急

A patient with convulsions visits a doctor who works at a sluggish pace – you are anxious but he is not

Lángzhōng 郎中 is a physician trained in herbal medicine. This expression is used to describe a situation where action is needed urgently but the person responds slowly.

Example

我饿死了，你还不做晚饭。真是急惊风遇见慢郎中。

我餓死了，你還不做晚飯。真是急驚風遇見慢郎中。

Wǒ èsǐ le, nǐ hái bú zuò wǎnfàn. Zhēn shì jíjīngfēng yùjiàn màn lángzhōng.

I'm starving to death, and you're still not making dinner. It's like a patient with a seizure seeing a doctor who refuses to be rushed.

39

Jià chuqu de gūniang, pō chuqu de shuǐ — nán shōuhuí

嫁出去的姑娘，泼出去的水——难收回

嫁出去的姑娘，潑出去的水 —— 難收回

A daughter married off or water that's been splashed – hard to get back

This expression is used to describe an irreversible development or decision.

Example

你知道你把钱借给他就像是嫁出去的姑娘，泼出去的水。为什么还要借给他？

你知道你把錢借給他就像是嫁出去的姑娘，潑出去的水。為甚麼還要借給他？

Nǐ zhīdao nǐ bǎ qián jiè gěi tā jiù xiàng shì jià chuqu de gūniang, pō chuqu de shuǐ. Wèishénme hái yào jiè gěi tā?

You know that lending money to him is like a daughter who's been married off or water that's been splashed. Why do you still lend him money?

Làiháma xiǎng chī tiān'é ròu — chī xīn wàng xiǎng

癞蛤蟆想吃天鹅肉——痴心妄想

40

癩蛤蟆想吃天鵝肉 ——癡心妄想

A toad wanting to eat a swan's flesh – wishful thinking or unrealistic aspirations

This expression is used to describe someone who cherishes foolish and exaggerated ideas.

Example

老陈又没学问又没钱还想娶名模陶小姐，真是癞蛤蟆想吃天鹅肉。

老陳又沒學問又沒錢還想娶名模陶小姐，真是癩蛤蟆想吃天鵝肉。

Lǎo Chén yòu méi xuéwen yòu méi qián hái xiǎng qǔ míng mó Táo xiǎojie, zhēn shì làiháma xiǎng chī tiān'é ròu.

Old Chen has neither learning nor money, yet he wants to marry the famous model, Miss Tao. He's like a toad lusting after a swan's flesh.

41

Lǎo tàitai de guǒjiǎobù — yòu chòu yòu cháng

老太太的裹脚布——又臭又长

老太太的裹腳布 ——又臭又長

An old lady's foot-binding rag – both smelly and long

This expression is used to characterize offensive or long-winded speeches or writings.

Example

这篇文章简直像老太太的裹脚布，看得我头疼。

這篇文章簡直像老太太的裹腳布，看得我頭疼。

Zhè piān wénzhāng jiǎnzhí xiàng lǎo tàitai de guǒjiǎobù, kànde wǒ tóuténg.

This article was like an old lady's foot-binding rag. Reading it gave me a headache.

Lǘ chún bú duì mǎ zuǐ — dá fēi suǒ wèn

驴唇不对马嘴——答非所问

42

驢唇不對馬嘴——答非所問

A donkey's lips do not match a horse's mouth – the answer doesn't correspond to the question

This saying is used when someone's answer or essay is not relevant to the question or topic.

Example

他问你北京的气候，你说了半天那儿的风俗习惯。简直是驴唇不对马嘴。

他問你北京的氣候，你說了半天那兒的風俗習慣。簡直是驢唇不對馬嘴。

Tā wèn nǐ Běijīng de qìhòu, nǐ shuō le bàntiān nàr de fēngsú xíguàn. Jiǎnzhí shì lǘ chún bú duì mǎ zuǐ .

He asked you about the climate in Beijing and you went on and on about the local customs there. It was like a donkey's lips not matching a horse's mouth.

43

Mábù shang xiù huā — dǐzi tài chà

麻布上绣花——底子太差

麻布上繡花——底子太差

Doing embroidery on burlap – the material is too coarse to accommodate such fine needlework

Burlap is a very rough material, so doing embroidery on it won't work. This xiēhòuyǔ refers to someone's education or background being inadequate for his position or job.

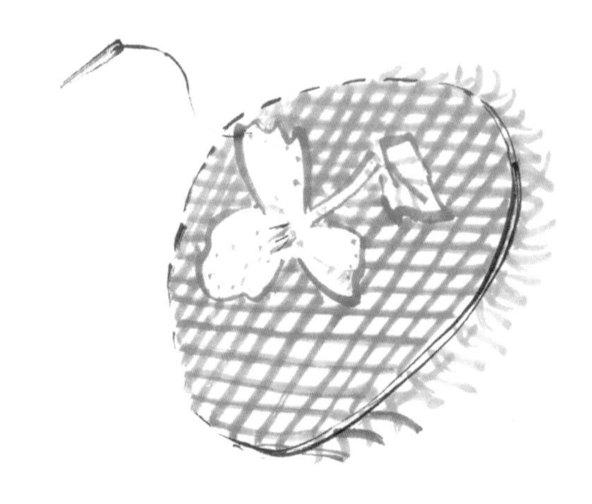

Example

难怪她做不好这件事，她既没有受过教育又没有经验。所以她是麻布上绣花。

難怪她做不好這件事，她既沒有受過教育又沒有經驗。所以她是麻布上繡花。

Nánguài tā zuò bù hǎo zhè jiàn shì. Tā jì méiyǒu shòu guo jiàoyù yòu méiyǒu jīngyàn. Suǒyǐ tā shì mábù shang xiùhuā.

No wonder she's done such a poor job. She has neither education nor experience. It's like trying to do embroidery on burlap.

Māo kū hàozi — jiǎ cíbēi

猫哭耗子——假慈悲

貓哭耗子——假慈悲

The cat cries for the rat – false sympathy or compassion

This xiēhòuyǔ is used to refer to someone as a hypocrite.

Example

我不信她是真心对我好。她那么做是猫哭耗子。

我不信她是真心對我好。她那麼做是貓哭耗子。

Wǒ bú xìn tā shì zhēn xīn duì wǒ hǎo. Tā nàme zuò shì māo kū hàozi.

I don't believe she is really nice to me. What she did was like the cat crying for the rat.

45

Mén fèng li kàn rén — bǎ rén kàn biǎn le

门缝里看人——把人看扁了

門縫裏看人 — 把人看扁了

Looking at someone through the crack between the door and its frame – underestimating people

Biǎn 扁 can mean flat or narrow, so that kàn biǎn le 看扁了 can mean either to underestimate someone or to see something narrowly or in only two dimensions.

Example

你不相信我能做这件事？别门缝里看人。

你不相信我能做這件事？別門縫裏看人。

Nǐ bù xiāngxìn wǒ néng zuò zhè jiàn shì? Bié mén fèng li kàn rén.

You don't believe I can do this job? Don't look at me through the crack between the door and its frame.

Pǎo le héshang, pǎo bù liǎo miào — jǐnguǎn fàngxīn ba

跑了和尚，跑不了庙——尽管放心吧

跑了和尚，跑不了廟——儘管放心吧

Though the monk may run away, the temple can't run with him – rest assured

This expression is used when you tell someone not to worry about a certain matter.

Example

别担心他没有付你房租，他父母还在这儿呢。跑了和尚跑不了庙。

別擔心他沒有付你房租，他父母還在這兒呢。跑了和尚跑不了廟。

Bié dānxīn tā méiyǒu fù nǐ fángzū, tā fùmǔ hái zài zhèr ne. Pǎo le héshang pǎo bù liǎo miào.

Don't worry about his not having paid your rent. His parents are still here. The monk may run away, but the temple remains.

47

Qián yǒu láng, hòu yǒu hǔ — jìn tuì liǎng nán

前有狼，后有虎——进退两难

前有狼，後有虎 — 進退兩難

There is a wolf in the front and a tiger in the back – difficult to advance or retreat

This expression is similar to the expression "between a rock and a hard place."

Example

美国政府要不要拯救美国三个大汽车公司的事情现在是前有狼，后有虎。

美國政府要不要拯救美國三個大汽車公司的事情現在是前有狼，後有虎。

Měiguó zhèngfǔ yào bu yào zhěngjiù Měiguó sān ge dà qìchē gōngsī de shì qing xiànzài shì qián yǒu láng, hòu yǒu hǔ.

As for bailing out America's three big automobile companies, the U.S. government is now facing a wolf in the front and a tiger in the back.

Qí mǎ bú dài biānzi — quán kào pāi mǎpì

骑马不带鞭子——全靠拍马屁

騎馬不帶鞭子 —全靠拍馬屁

Riding a horse without a whip – relying totally on patting the horse's rump

Pāi mǎpì also means "flattery" or "buttering [somebody] up." This xiēhòuyǔ is used sarcastically to ridicule someone as an apple-polisher.

Example

你知道张三为什么得到那么多奖金吗？是因为他是骑马不带鞭子。

你知道張三為甚麼得到那麼多獎金嗎？是因為他是騎馬不帶鞭子。

Nǐ zhīdao Zhāng Sān wèishénme dédào nàme duō jiǎngjīn ma? Shì yīnwèi tā shì qímǎ bù dài biānzi.

Do you know why Zhang San got such a big bonus? It was because he was riding a horse without a whip.

49

Qí lǘ zhǎo lǘ — hūn tóu hūn nǎo

骑驴找驴——昏头昏脑

騎驢找驢——昏頭昏腦

Looking for a donkey while riding it – confused

This expression is used when someone is muddleheaded or absent-minded.

Example

你是骑驴找驴。你看，你的眼镜就在你的头上。你还在找。

你是騎驢找驢。你看，你的眼鏡就在你的頭上。你還在找。

Nǐ shì qí lǘ zhǎo lǘ. Nǐ kàn, nǐ de yǎnjìng jiù zài nǐde tóu shang. Nǐ hái zài zhǎo.

You are looking for a donkey while riding it. Look, Your eyeglasses are on your head and you are still looking for them.

Ròu bāozi dǎ gǒu — yí qù bù huítóu

肉包子打狗——一去不回头

肉包子打狗 ——一去不回頭

Throwing a meat bun at a dog – one will never see it again

50

This expression is used when you lend money or something to someone without a realistic expectation of getting it back.

Example

你把钱借给他，我敢说就像是肉包子打狗。你最好考虑考虑。

你把錢借給他，我敢説就像是肉包子打狗。你最好考慮考慮。

Nǐ bǎ qián jiè gěi tā, wǒ gǎn shuō jiù xiàng shì ròu bāozi dǎ gǒu. Nǐ zuìhǎo kǎolǜ kǎolǜ.

Lending money to him, I dare say, is like throwing a meat bun at a dog. You'd best think it over.

51

Shā jī qǔ luǎn — dé bù cháng shī

杀鸡取卵——得不偿失

殺雞取卵 —得不償失

Killing the hen to get the eggs – the loss outweighs the gain

The meaning of this expression is obvious; failure to realize long-term loss for only a short-term gain.

Example

你做这么愚蠢的事情，就像是杀鸡取卵。

你做這麼愚蠢的事情，就像是殺雞取卵。

Nǐ zuò zhème yúchǔn de shìqing, jiù xiàng shì shā jī qǔ luǎn.

What you've done is so stupid. It's just like killing a hen to get the eggs.

Sān tiān dǎ yú, liǎng tiān shài wǎng — méi héngxīn

三天打鱼，两天晒网——没恒心

三天打魚，兩天曬網——沒恆心

Fishing for three days and drying the nets for two days – lacking perseverance

A fisherman should fish every day. This expression is used to criticize someone who doesn't keep working steadily on a job.

Example

你一定得天天锻炼。你不能三天打鱼，两天晒网。

你一定得天天鍛煉。你不能三天打魚，兩天曬網。

Nǐ yídìng děi tiāntiān duànliàn. Nǐ bù néng sān tiān dǎ yú, liǎng tiān shài wǎng.

You must exercise daily. You can't go fishing for three days and dry the nets for two days.

53

Shēng mǐ zhǔ chéng shú fàn — gǎi bù guòlái le

生米煮成熟饭——改不过来了

生米煮成熟飯——改不過來了

The rice has already been cooked – it can't be changed

Similar to "Black characters put down on white paper" above, this expression is used to say that something done can't be undone, i.e. don't cry over spilled milk.

Example

你现在不同意他们结婚还有什么办法。他们同居半年了。生米已经煮成熟饭了。

你現在不同意他們結婚還有甚麼辦法。他們同居半年了。生米已經煮成熟飯了。

Nǐ xiànzài bù tóngyì tāmen jiéhūn hái yǒu shénme bànfǎ. Tāmen tóngjū bànnián le. Shēng mǐ yǐjing zhǔ chéng shóu / shú fàn le.

If now you don't approve of their getting married, what can be done about it? They've been living together for half a year. The rice has already been cooked.

Shí chén dà hǎi — háo wú yīnxìn

石沉大海——毫无音信

石沉大海——毫無音信

A rock sinking into the sea – no news whatsoever

54

This expression is used to say someone or something has disappeared without a trace and nothing has been heard about it since.

Example

我的申请信已经寄去三个月了，像是石沉大海。

我的申請信已經寄去三個月了，像是石沉大海。

Wǒ de shēnqǐng xìn yǐjing jì qu sān ge yuè le, xiàng shì shí chén dà hǎi.

I sent the application in three months ago, it's like a rock sinking into the sea.

55

Tiānshàng de xīngxing — shǔ bù qīng

天上的星星——数不清

天上的星星 ——數不清

Stars in the sky – countless, innumerable

This expression conveys the idea of great quantity, something as innumerable as the stars in the sky.

Example

A: 美英有多少男朋友？

美英有多少男朋友？

Měiyīng yǒu duōshao nánpéngyou?

How many boyfriends does Meiying have?

B: 她的男朋友多得像天上的星。

她的男朋友多得像天上的星。

Tā de nánpéngyou duōde xiàng tiānshang de xīngxing.

Her boyfriends are as numerous as the stars in the sky.

56

Tiě gōngjī — yì máo bù bá

铁公鸡——一毛不拔

鐵公雞——一毛不拔

An iron rooster – can't pluck a feather

This expression ridicules a stingy person.

Example

我们都知道老范是铁公鸡。别想他会请客。

我們都知道老范是鐵公雞。別想他會請客。

Wǒmen dōu zhīdao Lǎo Fàn shì tiě gōngjī. Bié xiǎng tā huì qǐngkè.

We all know that Old Fan is an iron rooster. Don't expect him to treat us.

57

Tuō kùzi fàng pì — duō cǐ yì jǔ

脱裤子放屁——多此一举

脱褲子放屁——多此一舉

Take off one's pants to pass wind – do something that is superfluous

This expression is an earthy way of saying someone is doing something that isn't necessary.

Example

这件事你直接告诉我就好了，何必让别人转告我。这不是脱了裤子放屁吗？

這件事你直接告訴我就好了，何必讓別人轉告我。這不是脱了褲子放屁嗎？

Zhè jiàn shì nǐ zhíjiē gàosu wǒ jiù hǎo le, hébì ràng biéren zhuǎn gào wǒ. Zhè bú shì tuō le kùzi fàng pì ma?

You should have informed me of this matter directly. Why ask other people to pass it on to me? Isn't doing it this way like taking off your pants to pass wind?

Wáng pó mài guā — zì mài zì kuā

王婆卖瓜——自卖自夸

王婆賣瓜——自賣自誇

Old Lady Wang selling melons – to praise what one sells

This expression is roughly equivalent to "tooting one's own horn." Wáng pó mài guā 王婆卖瓜 can also be replaced with Lǎo Wáng mài guā 老王卖瓜 (Old Wang selling melons)

Example

刘先生老向别人夸耀他写的书，真是王婆卖瓜。

劉先生老向別人誇耀他寫的書，真是王婆賣瓜。

Liú xiānsheng lǎo xiàng biéren kuāyào tā xiě de shū, zhēn shì Wáng pó mài guā.

Mr. Liu is always bragging about his book to people. He is really like Old Lady Wang selling melons.

59

Wèng zhōng zhuō wūguī — pǎo bùliǎo le

瓮中捉乌龟——跑不了了

甕中捉烏龜——跑不了了

Catch a turtle in a jar – can't escape

This xiēhòuyǔ is often used to describe a sure thing.

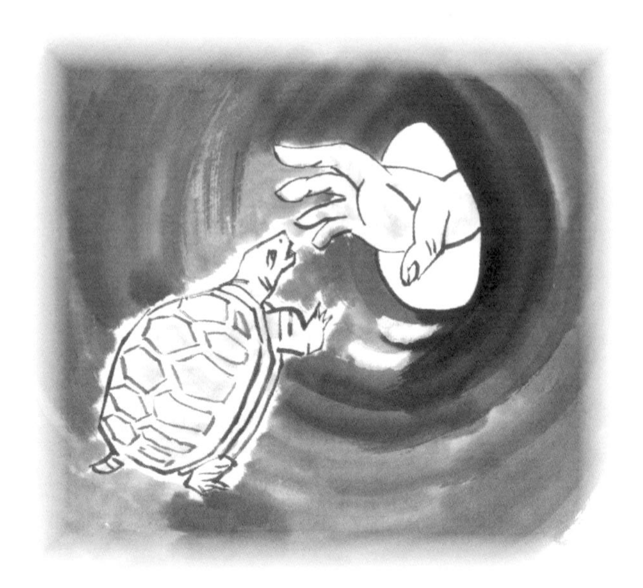

Example

这次我们有确实的消息，所以抓这些贩毒的人就如瓮中捉乌龟了。

這次我們有確實的消息，所以抓這些販毒的人就如甕中捉烏龜了。

Zhè cì wǒmen yǒu quèshí de xiāoxi, suǒyǐ zhuā zhè xiē fàndú de rén jiù rú wèng zhōng zhuō wūguī le.

This time we have reliable information, so arresting these drug dealers will be like catching a turtle in a jar.

Xiǎo cōng bàn dòufu — yīqīng'èrbái

小葱拌豆腐——一〔青〕清二白

小葱拌豆腐 —— 一〔青〕清二白

Scallion mixed with bean curd – perfectly clear and untainted

Scallion mixed with bean curd (with salt, soy sauce, and seasame oil) is a common Chinese dish, especially in Northern China. There are two colors in this dish: green (scallion) and white (bean curd) The character 青 qīng (green) and 清 (clear or innocent) have the same pronunciation. So, 一青二白 becomes 一清二白 . The phrase 一清二白 means perfectly clear or that someone's reputation is unblemished, that he (or she) is completely free of wrong-doing.

Example

(1) 这个案子已经是像小葱拌豆腐。法官判他无罪了。

這個案子已經是像小葱拌豆腐。法官判他無罪了。

Zhège ànzi yǐjing shì xiàng xiǎo cōng bàn dòufu. Fǎguān pàn tā wúzuì le.

From the start, this case was like scallion mixed with bean curd. The judge decided he was not guilty.

(2) 陈水扁说他没有贪污，他是小葱拌豆腐。你相信吗？

陳水扁說他沒有貪污，他是小葱拌豆腐。你相信嗎？

Chén Shuǐbiǎn shuō tā méiyǒu tānwū, tā shì xiǎo cōng bàn dòufu. Nǐ xiāngxìn ma?

Chen Shuibian [the former president of Taiwan] said that he wasn't guilty of corruption, that he was as clean as scallion mixed with bean curd. Do you believe it?

61

Xiān huā chā zài niúfèn shang — bái zāota le

鲜花插在牛粪上——白糟蹋了

鮮花插在牛糞上 ——白糟蹋了

Sticking a beautiful flower in cow dung – a total waste

This saying is used to describe a beautiful wife with an ugly husband (bái zāota le means "something is ruined or wasted")

Example

怎么这么又漂亮又年轻的女孩子嫁给了那个老头子？真是像鲜花插在牛粪上。

怎麼這麼又漂亮又年輕的女孩子嫁給了那個老頭子？真是像鮮花插在牛糞上。

Zěnme zhème yòu piàoliang yòu niánqīng de nǚháizi jià gěi le nèige lǎo tóuzi? Zhēn shì xiān huā chā zài niúfèn shang.

How can such an attractive young lady be married to that old man? It's really like sticking a beautiful flower in cow dung.

62

Xiāzi zhào jìngzi — kàn bú dào zìjǐ

瞎子照镜子——看不到自己

瞎子照鏡子——看不到自己

A blind person looking in the mirror – can't see himself

This expression is used to say one can't see one's own shortcomings or deficiencies.

Example

你呀，老觉得自己了不起，看不起别人，真是瞎子照镜子。

你呀，老覺得自己了不起，看不起別人，真是瞎子照鏡子。

Nǐ ya, lǎo juéde zìjǐ liǎobuqǐ, kànbuqǐ biéren, zhēn shì xiāzi zhào jìngzi.

You always think you are so terrific and look down on other people. It's really like a blind person looking in the mirror.

63

Xiā māo pèng shang le sǐ hàozi — qiǎo le

瞎猫碰上了死耗子——巧了

瞎貓碰上了死耗子 ——巧了

A blind cat coming upon a dead mouse – lucky

This xiēhòuyǔ is a humorous way to characterize a chance encounter or a lucky outcome.

Example

我看这次的行动这么顺利是运气好。瞎猫碰上了死耗子。

我看這次的行動這麼順利是運氣好。瞎貓碰上了死耗子。

Wǒ kàn zhè cì de xíngdòng zhème shùnlì shì yùnqi hǎo. Xiā māo pèng shang le sǐ hàozi.

I think that the operation having gone so smoothly was pure luck. Like a blind cat coming upon a dead mouse.

64

Xiǎo héshang niàn jīng — yǒu kǒu wú xīn

小和尚念经——有口无心

小和尚唸經——有口無心

An apprentice Buddhist monk reciting scriptures – not understanding or meaning what he says

The phrase is used of someone who doesn't mean or understand what he is saying.

Example

他说话就像小和尚念经。请你别在意。

他說話就像小和尚唸經。請你別在意。

Tā shuōhuà jiù xiàng xiǎo héshang niàn jīng. Qǐng nǐ bié zàiyì.

When he talks it is just like an apprentice Buddhist monk reciting scriptures. Please don't take what he said to heart.

65

Xuědì li gǔn qiú — yuè gǔn yuè dà

雪地里滚球——越滚越大

雪地裏滚球——越滚越大

Rolling a ball on snow-covered ground – the more you roll it the bigger it gets

This xiēhòuyǔ is used to indicate "snowballing" i.e. that the situation could get exponentially bigger.

Example

你想做股票的生意真的会像雪地里滚球一样吗？

你想做股票的生意真的會像雪地裏滚球一樣嗎？

Nǐ xiǎng zuò gǔpiào de shēngyi zhēn de huì xiàng xuědì li gǔn qiú yíyàng ma?

Do you think buying and selling stock really is like rolling a ball in the snow?

66

Yǎba chī huánglián — yǒu kǔ shuō bu chū

哑巴吃黄连——有苦说不出

啞巴吃黃連——有苦說不出

A mute eating a bitter herb – have a grievance but be unable to complain, be unable to express one's discomfort

Huanglian is an extremely bitter Chinese herbal medicine. The character kǔ 苦 can mean either bitter or suffering. Thus this saying is used to describe someone who is unable to express (or give vent to) his pain or is forced to suffer in silence.

Example

婆婆：	你们结婚三年了，怎么还没有孩子啊？
	你們結婚三年了，怎麼還沒有孩子啊？
Pópo:	Nǐmen jiéhūn sān nián le, zěnme hái méiyǒu háizi a?
Mother-in-law:	You have been married for three years, how come you still don't have any children?
媳妇 / 婦：	你别怪我。你最好去问你儿子。我是哑巴吃黄连啊。
	你別怪我。你最好去問你兒子。我是啞巴吃黃連啊。
Xífù:	Nǐ bié guài wǒ. Nǐ zuìhǎo qù wèn nǐ érzi. Wǒ shì yǎba chī huánglián a.
Daughter-in-law:	Don't put the blame on me. You'd better ask your son about this. I'm like a mute person eating a bitter herb.

67

Yǎba chī jiǎozi — xīnli yǒu shù

哑巴吃饺子——心里有数

啞巴吃餃子——心裏有數

A mute person eating dumplings – knowing how many dumplings he has eaten

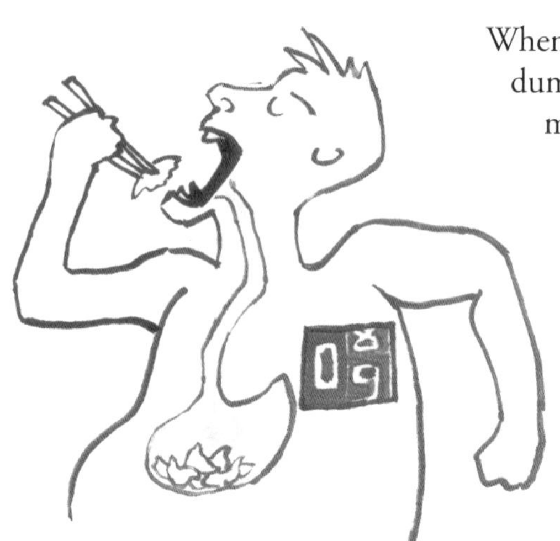

When a mute person eats dumplings, he knows how many dumplings he has eaten even though he cannot speak. This xiēhòuyǔ is used to describe someone who knows something very well, yet doesn't express (or articulate) it.

Example

虽然他不说话，可是我知道他什么都知道。他是哑巴吃饺子。

雖然他不說話，可是我知道他甚麼都知道。他是啞巴吃餃子。

Suīrán tā bù shuō huà, kěshì wǒ zhīdao tā shénme dōu zhīdao. Tā shì yǎba chī jiǎozi.

Although he hasn't spoken, I know he knows everything. He is like a mute person eating dumplings.

68

Yì zhī jiǎo cǎi liǎng tiáo chuán — sān xīn èr yì

一只脚踩两条船——三心二意

一隻腳踩兩條船 — 三心二意

Trying to stand in two boats on one leg – being of two minds

This expression is used to describe a person who can't make up his mind.

Example

你得快作决定。你不能一只脚踩两条船。

你得快作決定。你不能一隻腳踩兩條船。

Nǐ děi kuài zuò juédìng. Nǐ bù néng yì zhī jiǎo cǎi liǎng tiáo chuán.

You have to hurry up and make up your mind. You can't stand in two boats on one leg.

69

Zhàng èr héshang — mō bu zháo tóunǎo

丈二和尚——摸不着头脑

丈二和尚 ——摸不着頭腦

A monk who is one zhang and two chi tall – his head cannot be reached easily

The extended meaning of mō bu zháo tóunǎo is to describe something that is very hard to comprehend (i.e. one zhang and two chi in the above example is about 170 inches), just like a giant monk's head is difficult to reach.

Example

你说的是什么呀？我完全不懂你的意思。真叫我丈二和尚呀。

你說的是甚麼呀？我完全不懂你的意思。真叫我丈二和尚呀。

Nǐ shuō de shì shénme ya? Wǒ wánquán bù dǒng nǐ de yìsi. Zhēn jiào wǒ zhàng èr héshang ya.

What are you talking about? I am totally lost. It's just like asking me to reach as high as the head of a giant monk.

Zhè shān wàng zhe nà shān gāo — rénxīn bù zú

这山望着那山高——人心不足

這山望着那山高——人心不足

Seeing another mountain higher than this one – people are never satisfied

This expression is used to describe someone who is never satisfied with what he has. It's similar to the English expression, "The grass is always greener on the other side of the fence."

Example

我们很幸运有房子住。别这山望着那山高了。

我們很幸運有房子住。別這山望着那山高了。

Wǒmen hěn xìngyùn yǒu fángzi zhù. Bié zhè shān wàng zhe nèi shān gāo le.

We're very lucky to have a house to live in. Don't regard another mountain as higher than the one on which you are standing.

71

Zhǐshang tán bīng — wú jì yú shì

纸上谈兵——无济于事

紙上談兵 — 無濟於事

Talk war on paper – no practical effect

This expression is used to criticize someone for engaging in empty theorizing, for not being practical.

Example

你们所说的都是纸上谈兵。解决不了眼前的困难。

你們所說的都是紙上談兵。解決不了眼前的困難。

Nǐmen suǒ shuō de dōu shì zhǐshang tán bīng. Jiějué bù liǎo yǎnqián de kùnnan.

What you've said is merely talking war on paper. It cannot solve our present difficulties.

Zhǐ lǎohǔ — wài qiáng zhōng gān

纸老虎——外强中干

纸老虎——外強中乾

A paper tiger – outwardly strong but inwardly weak

This expression was used by Mao Zedong to describe American imperialism.

Example

毛泽东说美国是纸老虎。

毛澤東說美國是紙老虎。

Máo Zédōng shuō Měiguó shì zhǐ lǎohǔ.

Mao Zedong said that America was a paper tiger.

73

Zuǐ shang wú máo — bàn shì bù láo

嘴上无毛——办事不牢

嘴上無毛——辦事不牢

No hair around his mouth – not reliable at managing affairs

The man is too young to grow a beard and therefore not experienced enough to manage affairs. This expression is roughly equivalent to the English "still wet behind the ears."

Example

这件要紧的事情不能交给这么年轻嘴上无毛的人去办。

這件要緊的事情不能交給這麼年輕嘴上無毛的人去辦。

Zhè jiàn yàojǐn de shìqing bù néng jiāo gěi zhème niánqīng zuǐ shang wú máo de rén qù bàn.

You can't let such a young person, still beardless, handle such an important matter.

Zhú lánzi dǎ shuǐ — yì cháng kōng

竹篮子打水——一场空

74

竹籃子打水——一場空

Draw water with a bamboo basket – come up empty, nothing to show for his effort

This expression is used to describe a situation in which one has tried very hard but got nothing at the end, because a bamboo basket will leak and can't hold any water.

Example

王强把房子卖了，工作也辞了准备出国，可是没有得到签证，去不了了。真是竹篮子打水啊。

王強把房子賣了，工作也辭了準備出國，可是沒有得到簽證，去不了了。真是竹籃子打水啊。

Wáng Qiáng bǎ fángzi mài le, gōngzuò yě cí le zhǔnbèi chūguó, kěshì méiyǒu dédào qiānzhèng, qù bù liǎo le. Zhēn shì zhú lánzi dǎ shuǐ a.

Wang Qiang sold his house, quit his job and prepared to go abroad, but he didn't get his visa, so he can't go. Truly, it is like drawing water with a bamboo basket.

75

Zuò huǒjiàn shàng yuèqiú — yuǎn zǒu gāo fēi le

坐火箭上月球——远走高飞了

坐火箭上月球——遠走高飛了

Riding a rocket and flying to the moon – flying far and high

This expression describes someone who is always seems to be on the go.

Example

我不常看见我的孩子。他们都坐火箭上月球去了。

我不常看見我的孩子。他們都坐火箭上月球去了。

Wǒ bù cháng kànjian wǒ de háizi. Tāmen dōu zuò huǒjiàn shàng yuèqiú qù le.

I don't see my children very often. They are all riding a rocket and flying to the moon.

Part Two 第二部分

76

Bān mén nòng fǔ — zì bù liàng lì

班门弄斧——自不量力

班門弄斧——自不量力

Showing off his axe-handling skill before Ban's door – (displaying one's meager skill before an expert)

Lu Ban was a master carpenter. This saying, if it refers to the speaker, is an expression of modesty (as in the first example); if it is refers to someone else, it is satirical (as in the second example).

Example

(1) 我没有什么经验，在各位专家面前谈这个问题是班门弄斧。

我沒有甚麼經驗，在各位專家面前談這個問題是班門弄斧。

Wǒ méiyǒu shénme jīngyàn, zài gè wèi zhuānjiā miànqián tán zhège wèntí shì Bān mén nòng fǔ.

I have little experience, for me to discuss this matter with you experts would be like showing off my axe-handling skill before Ban's door.

(2) 他就做了三年的参议员就想竞选总统。真是班门弄斧。

他就做了三年的參議員就想競選總統。真是班門弄斧。

Tā jiù zuò le sān nián de cānyìyuán jiù xiǎng jìng xuǎn zǒngtǒng. Zhēn shì Bān mén nòng fǔ.

He has been senator for only three years and wants to run for president. Truly, it is like showing off one's axe-handling skill before Ban's door.

Bā Xiān guò hǎi — gè xiǎn shéntōng

八仙过海——各显神通

八仙過海——各顯神通

The Eight Immortals cross the sea – each has his/her own supernatural power

This xiēhòuyǔ is used to say that different individuals can accomplish the same task in different ways.

Legend has it that in ancient times there were Eight Immortals, each possessing special abilities and supernatural powers. One day the Eight Immortals headed out towards the Heavenly Palace. When they neared the edge of the Eastern Sea, they were greeted by a vast ocean with raging waves. Each used his/her own special supernatural power to cross safely.

Example

昨天晚上的球赛，每一个人都打得非常好。真是八仙过海。

昨天晚上的球賽，每一個人都打得非常好。真是八仙過海。

Zuótiān wǎnshang de qiú sài, měi yí ge rén dōu dǎde fēicháng hǎo. Zhēn shì Bā Xiān guò hǎi.

At last night's ball game everyone played really well. Truly, they were like the Eight Immortals crossing the sea.

78

Cǎo chuán jiè jiàn — mǎn zài ér guī

草船借箭——满载而归

草船借箭——滿載而歸

Straw boats borrowing arrows – (return from a rewarding journey)

This expression is a way of saying that one has been successful at getting or achieving something.

In the book *San Guo Yanyi* (*Romance of the Three Kingdoms*), Zhuge Liang sent twenty boats filled with straw dummies across the Yangzi River in a heavy fog. Cao Cao's soldiers shot at them; as a result, when Zhuge Liang retrieved the boats, they were filled with arrows.

Example

今天我买了很多减价的东西。真是草船借箭。好开心啊！

今天我買了很多減價的東西。真是草船借箭。好開心啊！

Jīntiān wǒ mǎi le hěn duō jiǎnjià de dōngxi. Zhēn shì cǎo chuán jiè jiàn. Hǎo kāixīn a!

Today, I bought a lot of things on sale. Truly, straw boats borrowing arrows. I'm so happy!

Dōngguō xiānsheng jiù láng — hǎo xīn méi hǎo bào

东郭先生救狼——好心没好报

東郭先生救狼——好心沒好報

Mr. Dongguo rescuing the wolf – (ill-rewarded for his kindness)

79

This expression is used of a person who (foolishly) shows kindness to an evil person. Mr. Dongguo is a character in "The Story of a Wolf in Zhongshan" by Ma Zhongxi of the Ming dynasty. In the story, Mr. Dongguo was nearly eaten by a wolf after he had helped it to hide from a hunter.

Example

我诚心诚意帮他忙。他说我是黄鼠狼给鸡拜年。真是东郭先生救狼。

我誠心誠意幫他忙。他說我是黃鼠狼給雞拜年。真是東郭先生救狼。

Wǒ chéngxīn chéngyì bāng tā máng. Tā shuō wǒ shì huángshǔláng gěi jī bàinián. Zhēn shì Dōngguō xiānsheng jiù láng.

I eagerly and sincerely wished to help him, but he said I was a yellow weasel wishing Happy New Year to a chicken. Truly, Mr. Dongguo rescuing the wolf. No reward for my kindness.

80

Gǒu yǎo Lǚ Dòngbīn — bù zhī hǎo rén xīn

狗咬吕洞宾——不知好人心

狗咬呂洞賓 —— 不知好人心

A dog snapping at Lü Dongbin (the first of the Eight Immortals) – (doesn't know a good man's heart)

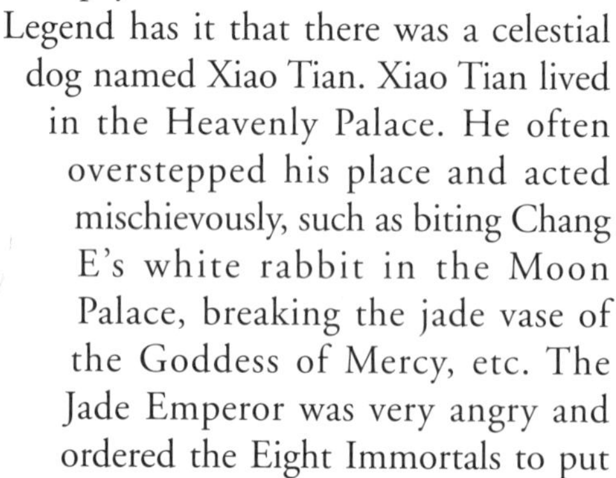

This expression is used to describe someone who repays kindness with evil.

Legend has it that there was a celestial dog named Xiao Tian. Xiao Tian lived in the Heavenly Palace. He often overstepped his place and acted mischievously, such as biting Chang E's white rabbit in the Moon Palace, breaking the jade vase of the Goddess of Mercy, etc. The Jade Emperor was very angry and ordered the Eight Immortals to put the dog to death. When Lü Dongbin saw the dog huddling and trembling incessantly, he took pity on it and wanted to let the dog get away quietly. The dog thought, since I am going to die anyway, I might as well go out fighting, so he jumped on Lü Dongbin and bit him. The bite was so severe that Lü Dongbin collapsed to the ground. When the seven other immortals came to help, the dog was nowhere to be found. Lü sighed, "My goodness has been repaid with evil."

Example

我再也不帮你的忙了。你真是狗咬吕洞宾。

我再也不幫你的忙了。你真是狗咬呂洞賓。

Wǒ zài yě bù bāng nǐ de máng le. Nǐ zhēn shì gǒu yǎo Lǚ Dòngbīn.

I'll never help you again. You're really like the dog that snapped at Lü Dongbin.

Guān Gōng miànqián shuǎ dà dāo — zì bù liàng lì

关公面前耍大刀——自不量力

關公面前耍大刀 —— 自不量力

Brandishing a sword before Guan Gong – (overestimating one's power)

Guan Gong 关公, a general of the Kingdom of Shu Han, was a master swordsman. If someone brandishes a sword before Guan Gong, it means he doesn't know his own limits. This saying, if it refers to the speaker, expresses humility or modesty (as in the first example); if it is used about someone else, it is a satirical remark (as in example two).

Example

(1) 我现在在您面前表演真是关公面前耍大刀。

我現在在您面前表演真是關公面前耍大刀。

Wǒ xiànzài zài nín miànqián biǎoyǎn zhēn shì Guān Gōng miànqián shuǎ dà dāo.

That I am now performing in front of you is really like brandishing a sword before Guan Gong.

(2) 你打得过他吗？真是关公面前耍大刀。

你打得過他嗎？真是關公面前耍大刀。

Nǐ dǎdeguò tā ma? Zhēn shì Guān Gōng miànqián shuǎ dà dāo.

Are you able to defeat him? You are really brandishing a sword before Guan Gong.

82

Guò hé chāi qiáo — bù liú hòu lù

过河拆桥——不留后路

過河拆橋 — 不留後路

Tearing down the bridge after crossing the river – leaving no way to return (burning one's bridges)

This expression is used to describe someone who turns on a benefactor as soon as help is no longer needed. This xiēhòuyǔ has its origin in a historical incident. Towards the end of the Yuan dynasty, a senior minister in the royal court submitted a report to Emperor Shun proposing the abolition of the imperial examination system for selecting men of talent, for he saw many faults in it. His proposal won the emperor's support. But another senior official, Xu Youren, was opposed to the idea. The emperor rejected Xu's views and even ordered him to announce the abolition of the imperial examination system, thus creating the false impression that Xu favored the abolition. Xu felt he had no choice but to obey against his own will. Some officials, not knowing the true situation, said of Xu sarcastically, "Xu Youren is a man who tears down a bridge after he crosses it," because Xu himself had entered on his official career by way of the imperial examination system.

Example

美国帮了那个国家那么多忙，现在他们反对美国，真是过河拆桥。

美國幫了那個國家那麼多忙，現在他們反對美國，真是過河拆橋。

Měiguó bāng le nèige guójiā nàme duō máng, xiànzài tāmen fǎnduì Měiguó, zhēn shì guò hé chāi qiáo.

The United States extended so much help to that country, now they have turned against her. This really is a case of tearing down the bridge after crossing the river.

83

Jiāng Tàigōng diào yú — yuàn zhě shàng gōu

姜太公钓鱼——愿者上钩

姜太公釣魚——願者上鈎

Lord Jiang's method of fishing – (only the willing get hooked)

The story of Jiāng Tàigōng's method of fishing is used as a metaphor for doing something of one's own free will. It is also used to describe one who willingly falls into a snare.

Towards the end of Shang dynasty, there was a man called Jiang Shang. People called him Lord (Taigong) He was known for his superb administration of state affairs. He served as a top official under King Zhou of Shang, but because he could not tolerate the wicked deeds of the king and his ruthless treatment of the people, he fled the court and became a recluse on the banks of the Weishui River

in Shaanxi Province. The site was in the territory of King Wen of Zhou. Jiang Taigong always fished by holding a straightened baitless hook suspended above the water. Jiang knew that King Wen was an ambitious man who longed to recruit the best personnel available. So every day he would sit fishing, waiting for King Wen to discover him. Lord Jiang passed his time in this way on the bank of the river for many years. It was not until he reached the age of eighty that his strange fishing method reached the ears of King Wen. Intrigued by this old man's eccentric ways, the king sent a soldier to find out what was going on.

When Lord Jiang saw the soldier coming, he paid no attention to him and kept fishing, while he shouted, "To hook, to hook! The big fish hasn't gone to the hook, and here comes a little shrimp to mess around with me!" The soldier returned and reported what he had seen and heard to the king. This time, the king sent over a high official to request Jiang's presence. Jiang again paid no attention to him and started to shout, "To hook, to hook! The big fish hasn't gone to the hook, and here comes a little fish to mess around with me!" The official returned and reported what his experience to the king. The king concluded that this man must be a man of exceptional ability. He therefore gathered all his officials and, carrying a special gift, made a trip to Weishui River to greet Lord Jiang. The king appointed Lord Jiang as prime minister of Zhou. From that time onward, Lord Jiang dedicated all his efforts to assisting King Wen in ruling the state.

Example

我没有强迫她做这件事。这是姜太公钓鱼。

我沒有強迫她做這件事。這是姜太公釣魚。

Wǒ méiyǒu qiǎngpò tā zuò zhè jiàn shì. Zhè shì Jiāng Tàigōng diào yú.

I didn't force her to do this job. This is Jiang Taigong's way of fishing.

84

Kǒngfūzǐ jiāo Sānzìjīng — dà cái xiǎo yòng

孔夫子教三字经——大才小用

孔夫子教三字經——大才小用

Confucius teaching the *Three Character Classic* – (wasting one's talent on a petty task)

Confucius was a great teacher. Sānzìjīng (the *Three Character Classic*) was a traditional children's primer. To ask Confucius to teach a children's primer would be a ridiculous use of his talent. This expression is used to characterize situations in which someone is overqualified for the task at hand.

Example

你是美国的硕士来教小学生，你真是孔夫子教三字经。

你是美國的碩士來教小學生，你真是孔夫子教三字經。

Nǐ shì Měiguó de shuòshì lái jiāo xiǎoxuéshēng, nǐ zhēn shì Kǒngfūzǐ jiāo *Sānzìjīng*.

You have a master's degree from the United States and now you're teaching primary school. You are really like Confucius teaching the *Three Character Classic*.

85

Kǒngfūzǐ de túdi — [xián] xiánrén

孔夫子的徒弟——〔贤〕闲人

孔夫子的徒弟 ——〔賢〕閒人

Confucius's disciple(s) – (virtuous person[s] / idle loafer[s])

All Confucius's disciples were supposedly virtuous persons 贤人. 贤人 and 闲人 (idle loafer) have the same pronunciation. This xiēhòuyǔ is a joking way of saying someone who is lazy or without a job.

Example

现在很多人失业了，都成了孔夫子的徒弟了。

現在很多人失業了，都成了孔夫子的徒弟了。

Xiànzài hěn duō rén shīyè le, dōu chéngle Kǒngfūzǐ de túdi le.

A lot of people have now been laid off and they have become Confucius's disciples.

86

Ná zhe jīmáo dàng lìngjiàn — xiǎo tí dà zuò

拿着鸡毛当令箭——小题大做

拿着雞毛當令箭——小題大做

Holding rooster feathers as if it were a token of authority – (making a big fuss over something trivial)

Lìngjiàn 令箭 was an arrow-shaped token of authority used in the army in ancient China.

Example

开妈妈的车有什么关系？你别拿着鸡毛当令箭。

開媽媽的車有甚麼關係？你別拿着雞毛當令箭。

Kāi māma de chē yǒu shénme guānxi? Nǐ bié názhe jīmáo dàng lìngjiàn.

What's the big deal about driving mother's car? Don't treat a rooster feather as if it were some ancient token of authority.

87

Qí lǘ kàn chàngběn — zǒu zhe qiáo

骑驴看唱本——走着瞧

騎驢看唱本——走着瞧

Riding a donkey while reading the lyrics – (wait and see)

A singer riding a donkey while reading song lyrics evokes an image of not being in a hurry and letting matters take their course.

Example

不要看不起他，他將来一定会比你成功。你不相信吗？骑驴看唱本，你们等着瞧吧。

不要看不起他，他將來一定會比你成功。你不相信嗎？騎驢看唱本，你們等着瞧吧。

Bú yào kànbuqǐ tā, tā jiānglái yídìng huì bǐ nǐ chénggōng. Nǐ bù xiāngxìn ma? Qí lǘ kàn chàng běn, nǐmen děng zhe qiáo ba.

Don't look down on him. In the future he will definitely be more successful than you. You don't believe it? Read the lyrics while riding the donkey, just wait and see.

88

Qiānlǐ sòng émáo — lǐ qīng qíngyì zhòng

千里送鹅毛——礼轻情意重

千里送鵝毛——禮輕情意重

Sending a goose feather a thousand miles – (the gift is light, but the sentiment is weighty)

This xiēhòuyǔ is now used as a polite formula when one gives a gift to someone.

During the Tang dynasty, there was a local official who had a precious swan. He sent a man named Mian Bogao to take the swan to the capital as a gift to the emperor. It was in June and the weather was very hot. Mian was afraid that the swan would die of the heat. One day when he reached the Mianyang Lake, he took the swan out of its cage and wanted to give the swan a bath. The swan burst out of his hands and flew away. All Mian had left on his hands was a single swan feather. He had no choice but to present the feather to the emperor and explain what had happened. He concluded with a poem. The last line of the poem was: 礼轻情义重，千里送鹅毛。Small as my gift is, rich it is with meaning. I have brought you this swan feather from thousands of miles away.

Example

这茶叶是我们家乡的土产。千里送鹅毛。请您收下。

這茶葉是我們家鄉的土產。千里送鵝毛。請您收下。

Zhè cháyè shì wǒmen jiāxiāng de tǔchǎn. Qiānlǐ sòng émáo. Qǐng nín shōu xia.

This tea is our hometown local product. We are sending a goose feather a thousand miles. Please accept it.

89

Sǐ mǎ dàng huó mǎ yī — shìshikàn

死马当活马医——试试看

死馬當活馬醫——試試看

Doctoring a dead horse as if it were still alive – (try and see)

This xiēhòuyǔ means that even if a situation is apparently hopeless, you can still make an effort to deal with it.

Guo Pu was a famous poet in the Western Jin dynasty. One day, he passed the residence of his friend General Zhao Gu. He decided to pay him a visit. Zhao refused to meet anyone, because he was mourning his horse. Guo told Zhao's gatekeeper that he could bring the horse back to life. The gatekeeper reported this to his master immediately. Zhao rushed out and asked, "Can you really revive my horse?" Guo said, "Yes. You must send some strong men to the woods and bring back a monkey-like creature." Zhao did just as Guo asked and his men brought back a monkey-like creature. Upon seeing the dead horse, this creature jumped onto the horse and blew air into the horse's nose. After a while, the horse woke up. General Zhao was overjoyed. He asked his servants to prepare a banquet for Guo and gave him a hundred taels of gold as a token of his gratitude.

Example

我没把握能修好你的电脑。死马当活马医。

我沒把握能修好你的電腦。死馬當活馬醫。

Wǒ méi bǎwò néng xiūhǎo nǐ de diànnǎo. Sǐ mǎ dàng huó mǎ yī.

I'm not sure if I can fix your computer. I would have to treat a dead horse as if it were alive.

90

Sūn Wùkōng de liǎn — shuō biàn jiù biàn

孙悟空的脸——说变就变

孫悟空的臉——說變就變

Sun Wukong's face – (change quickly)

This xiēhòuyǔ is used to describe unpredictable, sudden change.
Sun Wukong, the Monkey King, is one of the main characters in the novel Xī Yóu Jì (*Journey to the West.*) He has the power of 72 metamophoses, so he can change his face quickly and suddenly.

Example

你的主意真像孙悟空的脸。

你的主意真像孫悟空的臉。

Nǐ de zhǔyi zhēn xiàng Sūn Wùkōng de liǎn.

Your ideas are just like Sun Wukong's face.

91

Tiào jìn Huánghé xǐ bù qīng — yuānwang

跳进黄河洗不清——冤枉

跳進黃河洗不清——冤枉

Couldn't be washed clean after jumping into the Yellow River – (treated unjustly)

This xiēhòuyǔ is used to describe someone treated unjustly and unable to establish his innocence: it is impossible to be clean after jumping into the Yellow River because there is too much silt in it.

Example

我不知道这些毒品会在我家里。我现在真是跳进黄河洗不清。

我不知道這些毒品會在我家裏。我現在真是跳進黃河洗不清。

Wǒ bù zhīdao zhè xiē dúpǐn huì zài wǒ jiāli. Wǒ xiànzài zhēn shì tiào jìn Huánghé xǐ bù qīng.

I don't know why the narcotic drugs were in my house. Now, it's like I have jumped into theYellow River and can't be washed clean.

92

Shā jī yòng niú dāo — dà cái xiǎo yòng

杀鸡用牛刀——大才小用

殺雞用牛刀 —— 大才小用

Killing a chicken with a knife used to kill an oxen – (wasting great talent on a petty task)

This expression is used to describe someone who is overqualified for his job.

Confucius had a student named Zi You, who served as county magistrate in the small town of Wucheng. One day, Confucius with his students went to Wucheng. Confucius was very pleased knowing that Zi You had set up a school in such a small town. He heard students playing musical instruments, singing, and reading in the school yard. Confucius wanted to test Zi You, and said smiling, "Why must you use a butcher's knife to kill a chicken? Do you really need to promote education in such a small town?" Zi You answered, "You taught me that when an official is refined, he will develop a benevolent heart and love and treat others with respect and love; when the common people receive an education, they will understand how to follow orders and be law-abiding citizens."

Example

这点小事派那么高地位的人去，真是杀鸡用牛刀。

這點小事派那麼高地位的人去，真是殺雞用牛刀。

Zhè diǎn xiǎo shì pài nàme gāo dìwèi de rén qù, zhēn shì shā jī yòng niú dāo.

You sent such a high ranking official to do this petty task, it's like killing a chicken with a knife used to kill an ox.

Zhū Bājiè zhào jìngzi — lǐ wài bú shì rén

猪八戒照镜子——里外不是人

93

豬八戒照鏡子 —— 裏外不是人

Zhubajie (Pig) looks in the mirror – ([non-human inside and outside] blamed by both parties)

Zhubajie (Pig) is one of the main characters in the novel Xī Yóu Jì (*Journey to the West*). He has a pig's head and a human body. This expression is used to describe the situation where a mediator is attempting to intervene in a conflict or argument between two parties and both parties do not want or appreciate the intervention.

Example

你最好别管他们两个人的私事，否则一定是像猪八戒照镜子。

你最好別管他們兩個人的私事，否則一定是像豬八戒照鏡子。

Nǐ zuìhǎo bié guǎn tāmen liǎng ge rén de sīshì, fǒuzé yídìng shì xiàng Zhū Bājiè zhào jìngzi.

You'd better not involve yourself in their personal affairs; otherwise you will be like Pigsy looking in the mirror.

References

参考书 / 參考書

Běijīng Qiàopihuà Cídiǎn (xiūdìngběn). Yǔwén Chūbǎnshè. Zhōu Yīmín zhù, 1991.

《北京俏皮話詞典（修訂本）》。語文出版社。 周一民著，1991。

Dàzhòng Yǔdiǎn. Dàzhòng Wényì Chūbǎnshè. Xià Zhúfēng zhǔbiān, 2003.

《大眾語典》。大眾文藝出版社。 夏竹風主編，2003。

Hàn Yīng Cídiǎn. Yǔyán Wénhuà Dàxué Chūbǎnshè, 1997.

《漢英詞典》。語言文化大學出版社 1997。

《漢英歇後語詞典》*Hàn Yīng Xiēhòuyǔ Cídiǎn, A Chinese-English Dictionary of Enigmatic Folk Similes*. The University of Arizona Press, Tucson. By John S. Rohsenow, 1991.

Qiàopihuà 500 Tiáo. Huáyǔ Jiàoxué Chūbǎnshè. Lǐ Bǐngzé děng zhù, 2001.

《俏皮話 500 條》。 華語教學出版社。 李炳澤等著 2001。

Tōngyòng Xiēhòuyǔ Cídiǎn. Yǔwén Chūbǎnshè. Wēn Duānzhèng, Shěn Huìyún zhǔbiān, 2002.

《通用歇後語詞典》。 語文出版社。 溫端政，沈會雲主編，2002。

Tōngyòng Yànyǔ Cídiǎn. Yǔwén Chūbǎnshè. Wēn Duānzhèng, Shěn Huìyún zhǔbiān, 2004.

《通用諺語詞典》。 語文出版社。 溫端政，沈會雲主編，2004。

Xiēhòuyǔ Sìqiān Tiáo, Shànghǎi Wényì Chūbǎnshè. Sūn Zhìpíng, Wáng Shìjūn biān, 1983.

《歇後語四千條》。上海文藝出版社。 孫治平，王士均編，1983。

Xiēhòuyǔ Xīn Biān. Shāndōng Jiàoyù Chūbǎnshè. Tán Yǒngxiáng zhù, 1984.

《歇後語新編》。山東教育出版社。譚永詳著，1984。

Xīn Biān Xiēhòuyǔ. Guǎngxī Mínzú Chūbǎnshè. Zōng Háo biān, 2002.

《新編歇後語》。廣西民族出版社。宗豪編，2002。